Bloomers Island®

D1408730

Rosey Posey

and the

Perfectly Pink Radish

CYNTHIA WYLIE and
COURTNEY CARBONE

Illustrations by KATYA LONGHI

RODALE KiDS

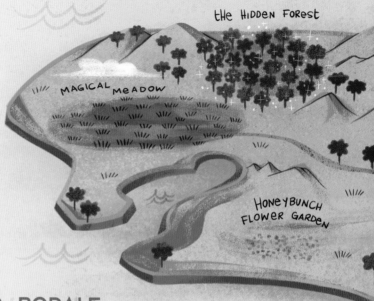

THE HIDDEN FOREST

MAGICAL MEADOW

HONEYBUNCH
FLOWER GARDEN

RODALE
KiDS
RODALEKIDS.COM

An imprint of Rodale Books
733 Third Avenue
New York, NY 10017
Visit us online at RodaleKids.com.

Text & art © 2018 Bloomers! Edutainment, LLC

All rights reserved. No part of this publication may be
reproduced or transmitted in any form or by any means,
electronic or mechanical, including photocopying, recording,
or any other information storage and retrieval system,
without the written permission of the publisher.

Rodale Kids books may be purchased for business or
promotional use or for special sales. For information,
please e-mail: RodaleKids@Rodale.com

Printed in China

Manufactured by RRD Asia 201802

Book design by Christina Gaugler and Ariana Abud

Library of Congress Cataloging-in-Publication Data is on file with the publisher.

ISBN 978-1-63565-054-9 paperback

Distributed to the trade by Macmillan

10 9 8 7 6 5 4 3 2 1 paperback

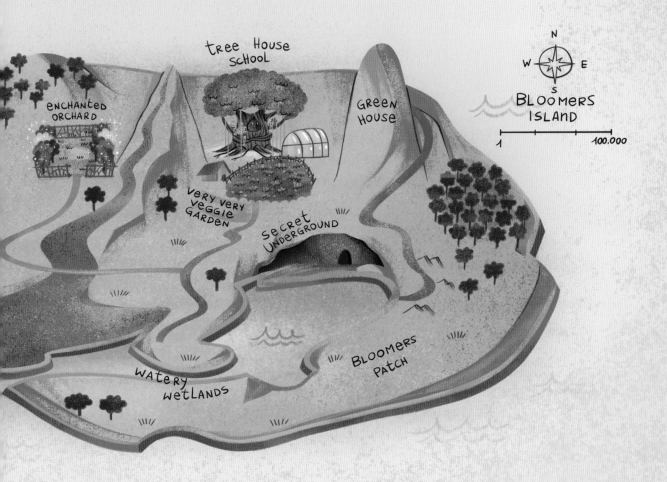

Dedicated to my daughter, Sophia Rose, the original Rosey Posey. Just remember that I love you *for* your idiosyncrasies, not in spite of them. You are even more perfect than a rose.

—C.W.

For budding green thumbs everywhere, that their hearts and minds may grow as magnificently as their gardens.

—C.B.C.

To my amazing husband and family for supporting and believing in me on this beautiful journey. Much love and thanks to everyone who follows my books and illustrations.

—K.L.

It was the start of a new school year on Bloomers Island. The headmaster of Tree House School, **Professor Sage**, was excited to teach his students, the Bloomers, all about the *wonderful world of gardening*.

"I have a special announcement today, class," Professor Sage said. "We are going to have a class contest. Each of you will grow your own vegetable, and in several weeks, we will see who has grown the best one."

Rosey Posey wanted to find an *extra* special vegetable to grow. She leafed through her textbook until she saw one that caught her eye—a plump pink vegetable called a radish!

After school, Rosey asked Professor Sage for radish seeds.

"An excellent choice!" he said, handing her the seeds and a book.

"What kind of radish would you like to plant? There are many different colors and varieties."

"How about a bright pink one?" Rosey replied. "That's my favorite color."

"I see," Professor Sage said.

"Then I would suggest
the Champion variety."

"Perfect!" Rosey replied.

"That sounds like the perfect
one to win the contest!"

Rosey brought the book up to the girls' dormitory and planted herself on her flowerbed.

She read all about radishes and wrote down everything she learned. She wanted to grow the most perfectly perfect plump pink radish to win the contest!

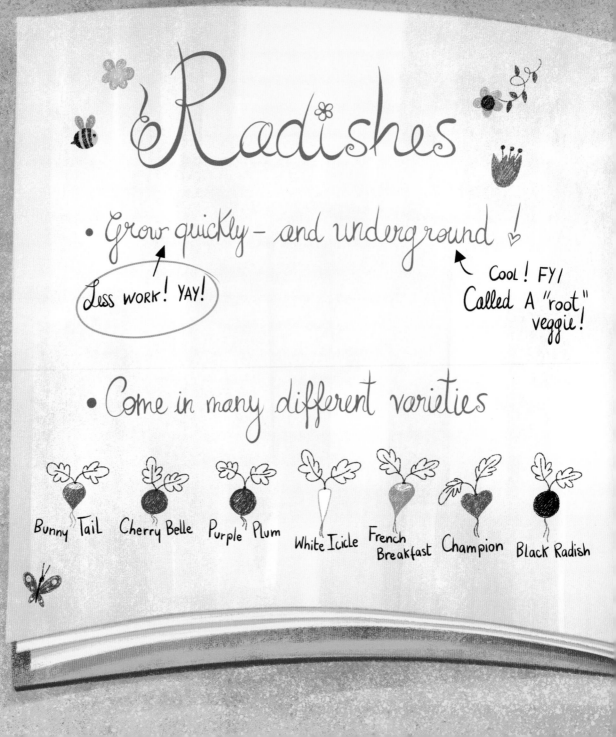

- Don't have many garden foes (pests who eat veggies!!!)

- OK to eat raw

Less cooking! Yum!

- Friendly

Grows well with others!

In the next few days, all of the students chose their vegetables for the contest. Rosey's friends **Violet**, **Daisy**, and **Lilly** could not wait to get started.

"Want to come plant your seeds in the garden with us, Rosey?" Violet asked.

"No thanks," Rosey replied. "I don't want to walk all the way down to the garden every day. I'm going to grow my radish in a pot on my windowsill instead."

From her upstairs window, Rosey watched her classmates playing and planting in the **Very Very Veggie Garden** below. They looked like they were having a lot of fun.

Rosey closed the curtain. She did not want to think about all the fun she was missing. Instead, she found a perfectly pink pot and planted her radish seeds.

Over time, Rosey watched her radish plant grow. She also watched her friends have more and more fun without her. As her radish grew bigger, so did the knot in her stomach.

Eventually, Rosey couldn't take it anymore. She decided to see if she could move her radish down to the garden to be with her friends.

"Professor Sage," Rosey asked. "Can I move my radish down to the garden?"

"Hmm," Professor Sage replied. "Radishes don't transplant easily, Rosey . . . but they *do* grow quickly, so you have time to grow more before the contest ends."

Rosey was thrilled. It wasn't too late to join her friends!

While she didn't like the idea of starting all over, she decided it was worth the extra effort to feel like part of the group again.

Rosey walked down to the garden, where her friend **Big Red** warmly welcomed her—by splashing her with the garden hose! Rosey laughed and enjoyed being back with her friends.

She knew she had made the right decision.

1. She dug holes in the shape of a heart.

2. She planted the seeds.

3. She added compost.

4. She watered the seeds.

Over the next several weeks, Rosey's radish plants grew big and strong. Soon the veggies began to poke out of the soil from where they were growing below!

She gently pulled one out. It was almost as big as her hand.
The radishes were ready to harvest!

Rosey put all of the radishes into a basket. She brought them into the kitchen, where she saw Professor Sage was making his famous macaroni and cheese.

"The radishes look wonderful, Rosey!" Professor Sage said proudly.

They trimmed and sliced the vegetables and fried them in a pan. They then added them to Professor Sage's macaroni and cheese. It was a perfect combination!

Together, they ate the radish macaroni and cheese.

"I'm glad all that hard work paid off," Rosey said. "This is my new favorite dish!"

"That's great," Professor Sage laughed. "Because there are plenty of leftovers!"

After they cleaned up, Professor Sage showed Rosey a special trick.

"If you put the radishes in a bowl of cool water in the fridge, they last longer," he said.

"Hooray!" Rosey exclaimed. "More radishes tomorrow!"

The next day, Rosey told her whole class all about her favorite vegetable. She held up the most perfectly pink radish.

The Bloomers munched on fresh slices of raw radish as she spoke.

"Well done, Rosey!" Professor Sage said when she had finished. "You have worked very hard—twice— and have earned the award for Most Colorful Vegetable!"

Everyone cheered, and Rosey's proud face turned the color of her prize veggies.

Rosey Posey's
Perfectly Pink Dip

Ingredients

1 bunch fresh pink radishes

8-ounce package cream cheese

¼ cup plain Greek or coconut milk yogurt

1 tablespoon Italian seasoning

2 teaspoons minced garlic

½ teaspoon sea salt

2 or 3 fresh basil leaves, finely chopped

Directions

1. With a grownup's supervision, preheat the oven to 375 degrees F.

2. Remove the stems and cut the radishes into quarters, then spread them on a parchment paper-lined baking sheet.

3. Place the baking sheet in the oven and remove after 20 to 25 minutes or until the radishes start to turn translucent.

4. Using a blender or food processor, combine the cream cheese and roasted radishes.

5. Add yogurt, Italian seasoning, minced garlic, sea salt, and basil. Blend well.

6. Enjoy your delicious and perfectly pink dip with baby carrots and celery, or wrap it in a tortilla with sliced turkey and fresh spinach!